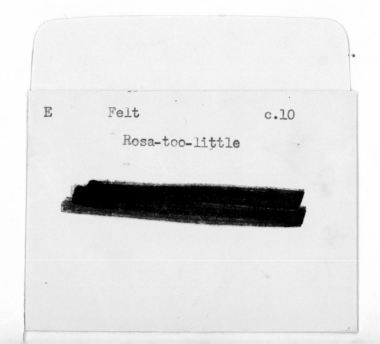

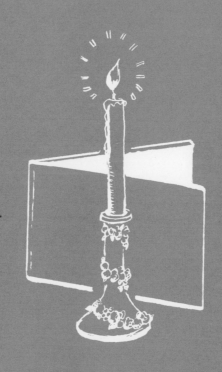

ROSA-TOO-LITTLE

story and pictures

by **SUE FELT**

DOUBLEDAY & COMPANY, INC.
GARDEN CITY, NEW YORK

ROSA-TOO-LITTLE

It was winter. The snow was piled in shapeless mounds along 110th Street.

But it wasn't the snow that bothered Rosa as she followed Margarita up the library steps into the warm indoors.

For as long as she could remember Rosa had been following her big sister, Margarita, to the library.

And every time Rosa waited while Margarita returned her books.

And every time she waited Rosa was sad. She wanted very much to have books of her own to return.

"Please, Margarita," she would say, "when can I join?"

"You are too little, Rosa. You have to write your name and get a card before you can take books out."

"It is always the same. Last winter I was too little. Last summer I was too little. Why am I always too little to have my own books?" Rosa sighed.

Rosa was big enough to help her mother at home while Margarita and Antonio were at school. But whenever Margarita came from school to take her to the library, Rosa was ready.

Always before Margarita chose new books she would hold Rosa up to press her face against the cool glass to look into that small other world of the PEEP SHOW.

"Oh, there is Peter Rabbit in bed," Rosa would say, "and there is Mrs. Rabbit making him some Camomile Tea and Flopsy, Mopsy, and Cottontail are eating bread and milk and blackberries."

On Fridays Margarita and Antonio went to STORY HOUR upstairs while Rosa, who was too little, sat in the READING ROOM looking at the Picture Books. She looked at the pictures until she knew every one by heart. This made Rosa sad, too. She was certain that if she could only have her own library card and take home her own books she would be able to read them. She wanted so much to go to STORY HOUR, too, and hear the library teacher tell fairy tales. Sometimes Margarita told Rosa the stories or read them to her at home. But Rosa knew it was not quite the same as hearing them at STORY HOUR. She was sure she must be nearly big enough to make a wish and help blow out the candle after STORY HOUR. Antonio had told her about that part, too.

"Oh, how I would like to do that. Why am I always too little?" Rosa sighed.

The snow melted. After light spring rains the trees in Central Park were fringed with baby green leaves.

Margarita carried her jump rope to school and often played double Dutch on the sidewalks in the evenings as the nights grew warmer.

And Rosa was too little for jump rope.

When Margarita wasn't jumping rope she was roller skating. And Mother said Rosa was too little for roller skates.

It seemed to Rosa she was too little for everything. Antonio and his friends once again were training their pigeons on the rooftops. Antonio and his friends didn't want her on the roof. And Antonio was too busy to take her to the library. No one would take her to the library. And that was what Rosa wanted to do most of all.

She was sad.

Rosa begged and begged her mother to let her go alone to the library.

Finally one day her mother said yes.

Rosa could go all by herself. She remembered to wait for the green lights crossing the street. She remembered to wait in line. She was very proud to do it all alone.

But when at last she reached the desk and the library teacher asked for her books, Rosa suddenly remembered something else.

Rosa Maldonado did not have any books; she did not even have a library card. She was too little to join. Poor little Rosa covered her face, pushed her way out of the line, and ran down the stairs, out the door, and all the way home.

"Rosa, little dear, what is the matter, *chiquita?*" her mother asked. Rosa sobbed louder, but at last her mother understood.

"Rosa," she comforted, "we will make a plan. a secret for you and me!"

And Rosa was not quite so sad!

The next day was hot, but Rosa and her mother didn't mind. They started their plan.

All through the long, hot, city summer Rosa worked on her plan except for the days when the street-cleaning men turned on the water hydrant, *the Pompa*, Rosa, Margarita, and Antonio called it. Then they rushed through the fast, cold spray of water. The pavement was cool on the soles of their feet.

Most of the children forgot about books, but not Rosa.

Sometimes in the afternoon Margarita took Rosa to hear the Picture Books read in the library. Everything was quiet in the summer. There were not so many children, for some of them were in camp and some were in the country and all the rest were too hot and sticky to do much of anything.

Rosa listened to the stories and smiled inside with her secret.

And every day Rosa worked on her plan in a special corner at home so that Margarita and Antonio wouldn't guess.

One day Mama said:

"When school starts in September, Rosa may go with Margarita and Antonio."

Then Rosa smiled. She was not too little any more. She could hardly wait.

The last day before school was to begin the little penny merry-go-round came. *La machina,* the children called it. Everyone on 110th Street who had pennies had a ride, and the others followed the music. But they weren't so happy as when *la machina* had been there in the spring. Playtime was over—no more long days of jump rope, marbles, skating, and stoopball.

But Rosa skipped with joy.

On Monday school started, and Rosa walked with Margarita and Antonio—quiet and proud. It was very exciting to be in school, but there was something else Rosa wanted to do, too.

At three o'clock she waited by the playground gate till Margarita and Antonio came out and then Rosa pulled her sister's hand.

"Margarita, Margarita, today may I go?"

"Rosa, what are you talking about? How do you like school?" said Margarita.

"It's wonderful. But Margarita, today may I go to the library with you?" asked Rosa, still pulling her sister's hand.

"But Rosa," said Margarita, "why today? I have homework to do."

"Please, Margarita." And finally Margarita gave in to Rosa's pleading and they went together to the library.

Lots of boys and girls were back again to get their cards after the summer. Soon Rosa's turn came.

"What do you want, Rosa?" asked the librarian, who had seen Rosa so many times she knew her name.

"I want to join, please," said Rosa.

"Oh, but Rosa, you are very little. You must be able to write your name you know."

"I can write my name," Rosa said proudly.

The library lady smiled and took a white slip of paper from a drawer, dipped a pen in the inkwell, and said: "Write your name on this line, Rosa."

Rosa held tight to the pen and carefully, carefully made the letters

ROSA "MALTIANA

The pen scratched. Rosa wasn't used to ink, and she wasn't sure the librarian could read her name, but when Rosa looked up, the library lady smiled.

"That's fine, Rosa," she said.

"Why, Rosa," Margarita said, "that's wonderful!" and she wrote in the address and school and Rosa's grade and age.

"Rosa, take this home and have your mother fill out the other side, then bring it back," the librarian said.

Rosa ran down the stairs and out the door. She ran all the way home and into the kitchen where her mother was preparing dinner.

"Mama, Mama, I joined, I joined! I wrote my name and you must sign the paper so I can get my card."

Her mother smiled proudly and kissed Rosa's hot little face. She signed her name and Rosa's father's name on the back of the paper.

The librarian was surprised to see Rosa back so soon.

"I ran," Rosa said, and showed her mother's name on the paper. Then the librarian gave Rosa a blue slip of paper and Rosa wrote her name again. All the time Rosa saw her name on a brand-new card. It would be all her own. The library teacher helped her read the pledge:

When I write my name in this book, I promise to take good care of the books I use in the library and at home and to obey the rules of the library.

Then Rosa stood on a stool and wrote her name in the big book. That was the best moment of all, because now Rosa Maldonado's name was in the book, the big black book where all the other children who could write had signed their names.

She listened to the rules carefully, although she already knew them. She promised to take good care of her books and to bring them back on time and always to have her hands clean!

Then Rosa walked over to the EASY BOOKS and found the two books she wanted. She knew just where to find them.

Rosa then waited in line to have her books stamped. She smiled back at the library teacher.

Then she walked down the library stairs and
out into the brisk evening. She squeezed her
very own books.

"I am not too little any more," said Rosa.

She was very happy.